Konte Chameleon Fine, Fine, Fine!

A West African Folktale

This book is dedicated to my nieces and nephews:
Doria, Stephanie, Margharita, Alicia, Ben, Jackie, Brian, Tory,
Rachel, and Jesse. I'd also like to thank my husband, Joe, and Yao Gozo,
who first shared this tale with me.

—C. K.

To my mother, whose support towards me never flinched, and to Françoise
and Marthe, my beloved daughters.

—C. E.

Text copyright © 1997 by Cristina Kessler
Illustrations © 1997 by Christian Arthur Kingue Epanya

Published by Caroline House
Boyds Mills Press, Inc.
A Highlights Company
815 Church Street
Honesdale, Pennsylvania 18431
Printed in Hong Kong

Publisher Cataloging-in-Publication Data
Kessler, Cristina.
    Konte Chameleon, Fine, Fine, Fine! /retold by Cristina Kessler ; illustrated by Christian Arthur Kingue Epanya.—1st ed.
[32]p. : col.ill. ; cm.
Summary : An retold folktale about a chameleon who wonders why he changes color.
ISBN 1-56397-181-X
1. Chameleons—Fiction—Juvenile literature. 2. Imagination—Fiction—Juvenile literature. [1. Chameleons—fiction.
2. Imagination—Fiction.] I. Epanya, Christian Arthur Kingue, ill. II. Title.
    [E]—dc20   1997   AC   CIP
Library of Congress Catalog Card Number 95-80781

First edition, 1997
Book designed by Tim Gillner
The text of this book is set in 16-point Post Antiqua.
The illustrations are done in acrylics.

10 9 8 7 6 5 4 3 2 1

KONTE CHAMELEON
FINE, FINE, FINE!

A WEST AFRICAN FOLKTALE

• Retold by Cristina Kessler •

Illustrated by Christian Epanya

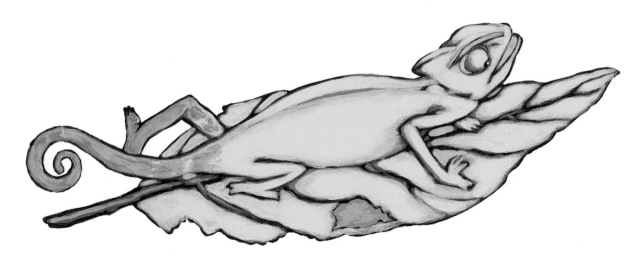

Boyds Mills Press

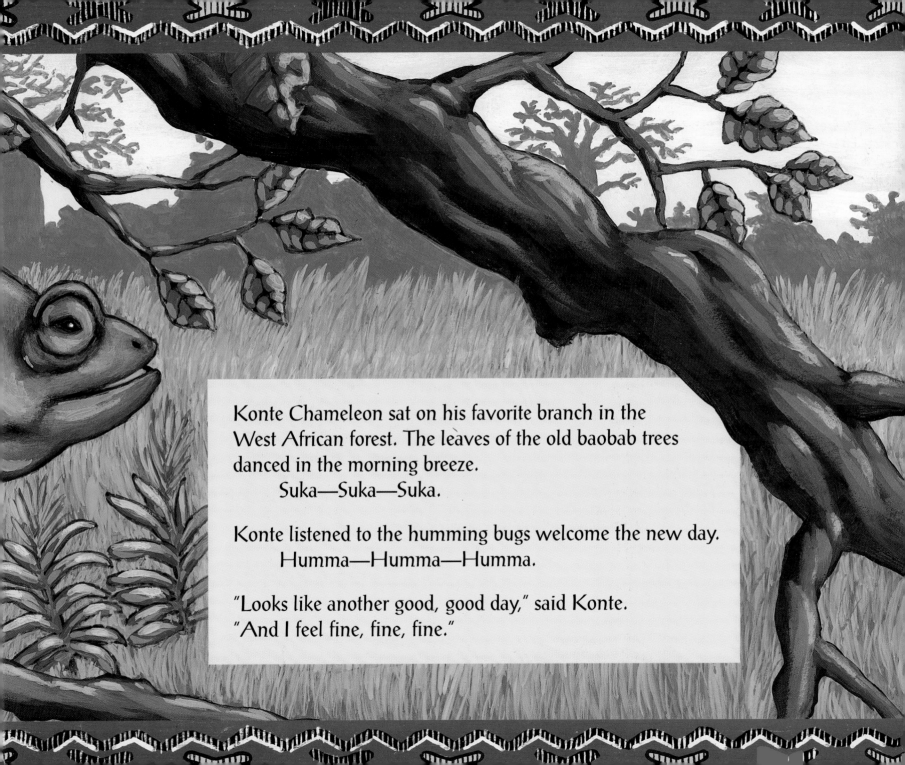

Konte Chameleon sat on his favorite branch in the West African forest. The leaves of the old baobab trees danced in the morning breeze.
Suka—Suka—Suka.

Konte listened to the humming bugs welcome the new day.
Humma—Humma—Humma.

"Looks like another good, good day," said Konte.
"And I feel fine, fine, fine."

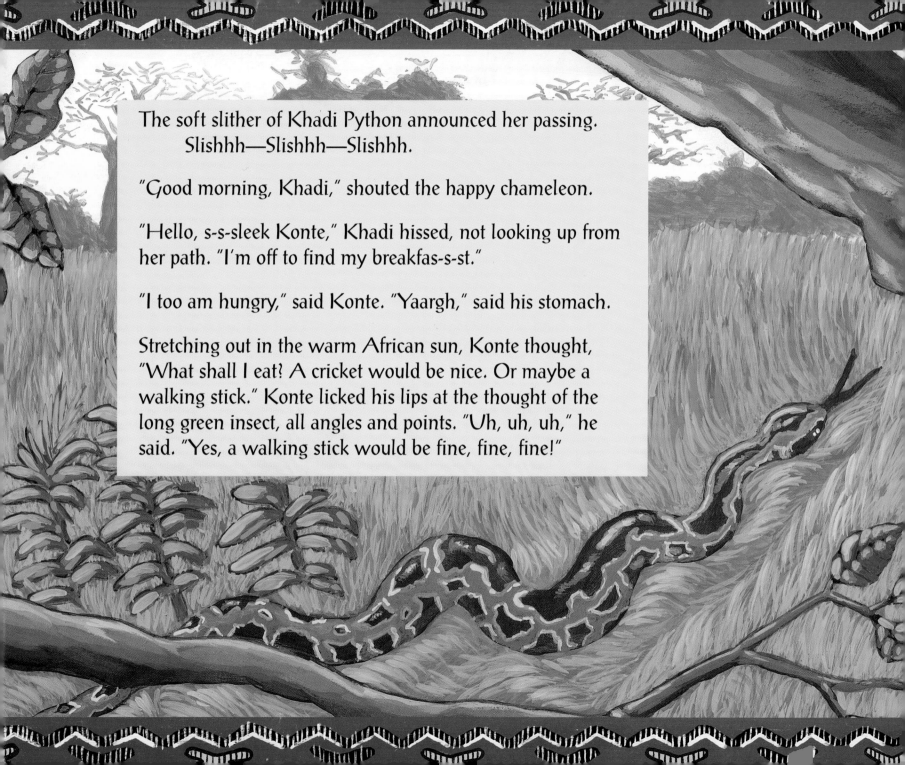

The soft slither of Khadi Python announced her passing. Slishhh—Slishhh—Slishhh.

"Good morning, Khadi," shouted the happy chameleon.

"Hello, s-s-sleek Konte," Khadi hissed, not looking up from her path. "I'm off to find my breakfas-s-st."

"I too am hungry," said Konte. "Yaargh," said his stomach.

Stretching out in the warm African sun, Konte thought, "What shall I eat? A cricket would be nice. Or maybe a walking stick." Konte licked his lips at the thought of the long green insect, all angles and points. "Uh, uh, uh," he said. "Yes, a walking stick would be fine, fine, fine!"

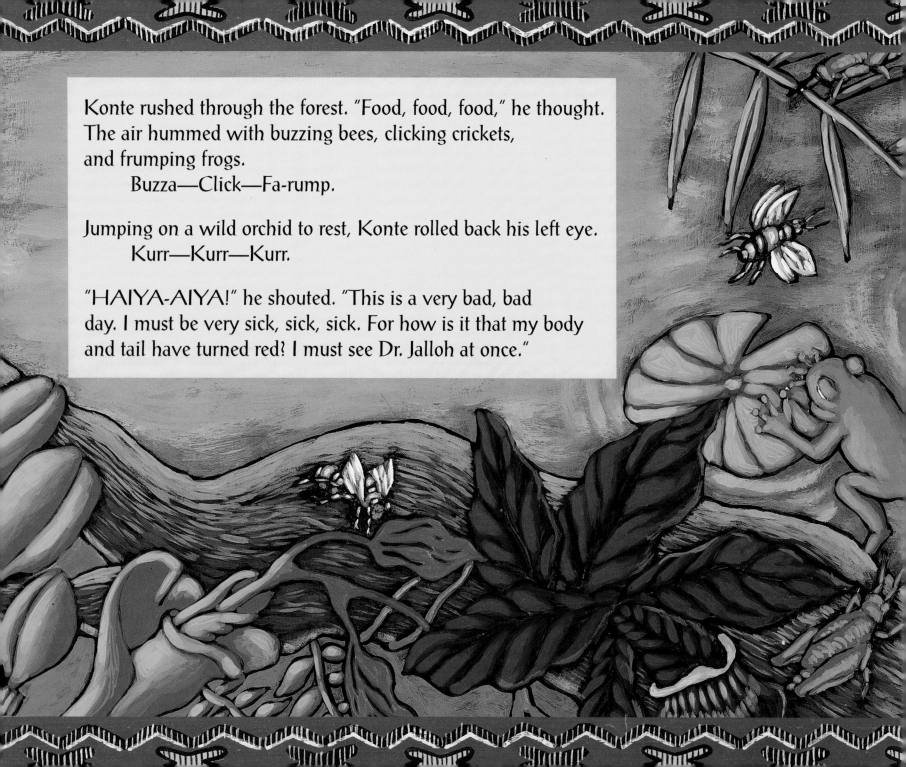

Konte rushed through the forest. "Food, food, food," he thought. The air hummed with buzzing bees, clicking crickets, and frumping frogs.
    Buzza—Click—Fa-rump.

Jumping on a wild orchid to rest, Konte rolled back his left eye.
    Kurr—Kurr—Kurr.

"HAIYA-AIYA!" he shouted. "This is a very bad, bad day. I must be very sick, sick, sick. For how is it that my body and tail have turned red? I must see Dr. Jalloh at once."

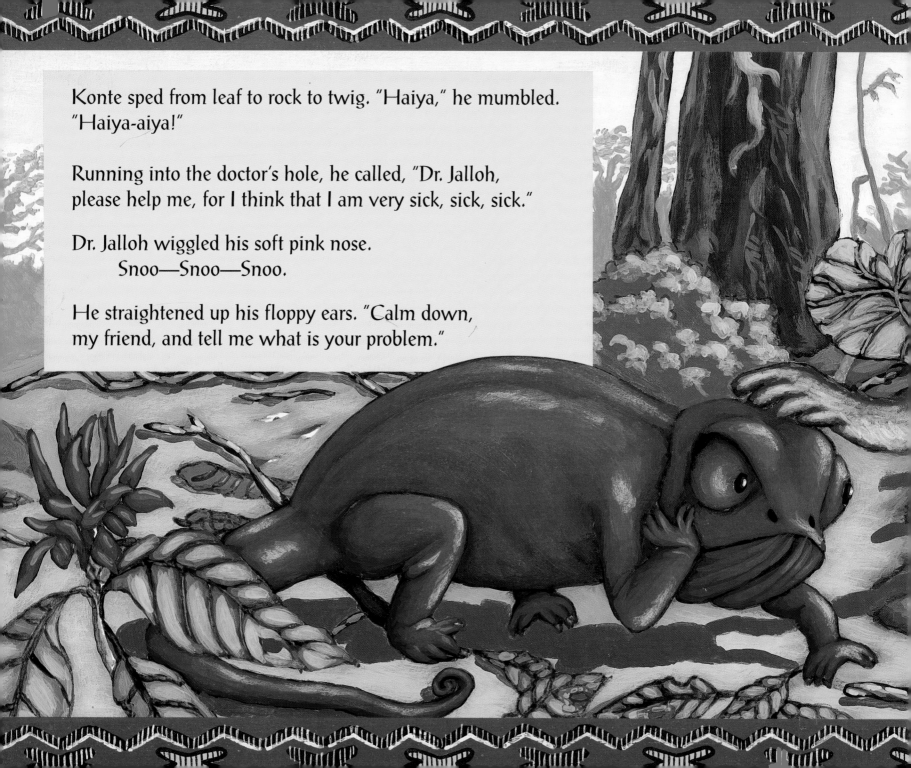

Konte sped from leaf to rock to twig. "Haiya," he mumbled.
"Haiya-aiya!"

Running into the doctor's hole, he called, "Dr. Jalloh,
please help me, for I think that I am very sick, sick, sick."

Dr. Jalloh wiggled his soft pink nose.
    Snoo—Snoo—Snoo.

He straightened up his floppy ears. "Calm down,
my friend, and tell me what is your problem."

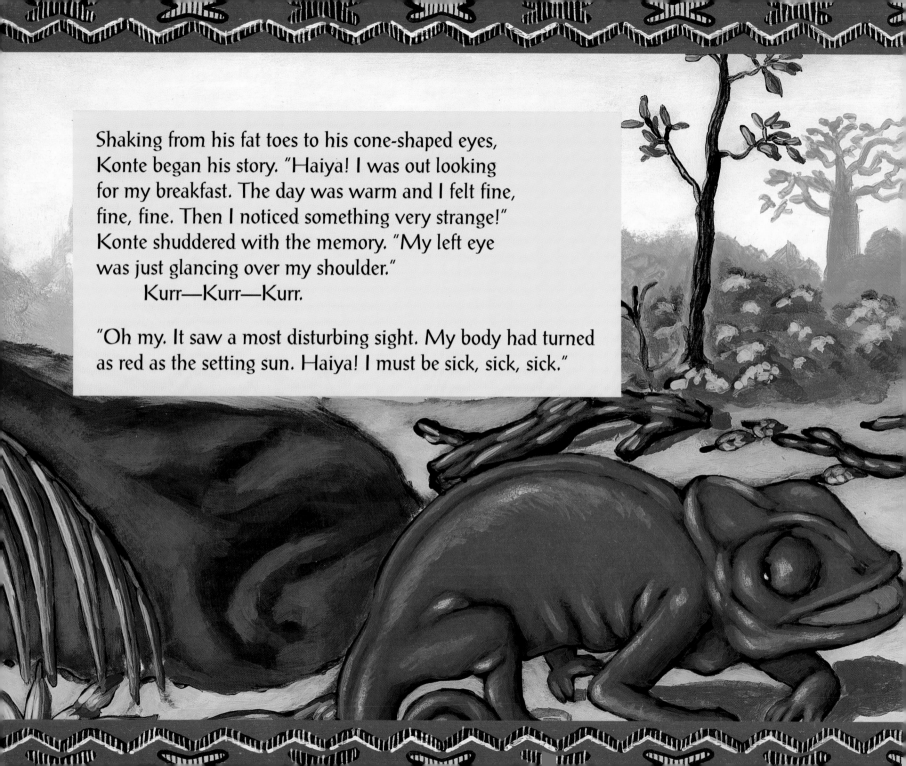

Shaking from his fat toes to his cone-shaped eyes, Konte began his story. "Haiya! I was out looking for my breakfast. The day was warm and I felt fine, fine, fine. Then I noticed something very strange!" Konte shuddered with the memory. "My left eye was just glancing over my shoulder."

Kurr—Kurr—Kurr.

"Oh my. It saw a most disturbing sight. My body had turned as red as the setting sun. Haiya! I must be sick, sick, sick."

"Let me examine you," said Dr. Jalloh. "Open your mouth and stick out your tongue."

Flinging out his tongue—THWACK!—Konte caught a passing fly.

The doctor nodded his furry head. "Hummmm. The tongue is fine."

Then Doctor Jalloh checked Konte's eyes.
Konte rolled the right eye up.
    Kurr—Kurr—Kurr.

While he rolled the left eye down.
    Kurr—Kurr— Kurr.

"Your eyes are fine, too," the doctor said.
"Now grab this twig. I want to check your feet."

Konte's fat toes on each foot wrapped around the twig.
    Whuut—Whuut. Whuut—Whuut.

"Your feet are fine," said the doctor.
"And so, Konte, where were you when your body turned red?"
asked Doctor Jalloh.

"HAIYA! On a wild red orchid," answered the
trembling lizard. "Tell me, Dr. Jalloh, am I very sick, sick, sick?"

Doctor Jalloh wiggled his pink nose.
　　　Snoo—Snoo—Snoo.

He placed his fluffy paw on the chameleon's shoulder.
"Come along. There is something I must show you."

Konte fixed wide eyes on the doctor.
　　　Kurr—Kurr—Kurr.
　　　Kurr—Kurr—Kurr.

He prepared himself for the worst. "Haiya-aiya!
What can be wrong with me?" he said in a
quaky, shaky voice.

"Climb onto that yellow flower," said Doctor Jalloh.
"Now look at your tail. What color are you?"

Back went Konte's right eye.
    Kurr—Kurr—Kurr.

"I am as yellow as a ripe banana. Oh, I must be
very sick, sick, sick."

"Now, now, my friend," said Dr. Jalloh.
"Please jump on that brown rock."

Konte jumped. Back went his left eye.
　　　　Kurr—Kurr—Kurr.

"B-b-b-brown as a coconut shell," he said.

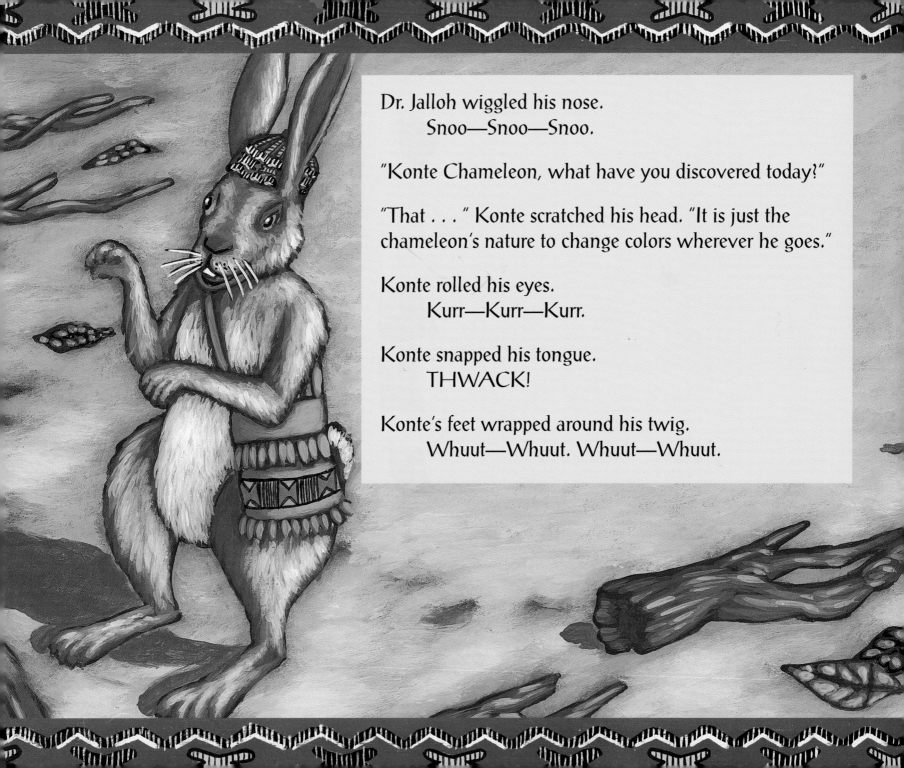

Dr. Jalloh wiggled his nose.
    Snoo—Snoo—Snoo.

"Konte Chameleon, what have you discovered today?"

"That . . ." Konte scratched his head. "It is just the chameleon's nature to change colors wherever he goes."

Konte rolled his eyes.
    Kurr—Kurr—Kurr.

Konte snapped his tongue.
    THWACK!

Konte's feet wrapped around his twig.
    Whuut—Whuut. Whuut—Whuut.

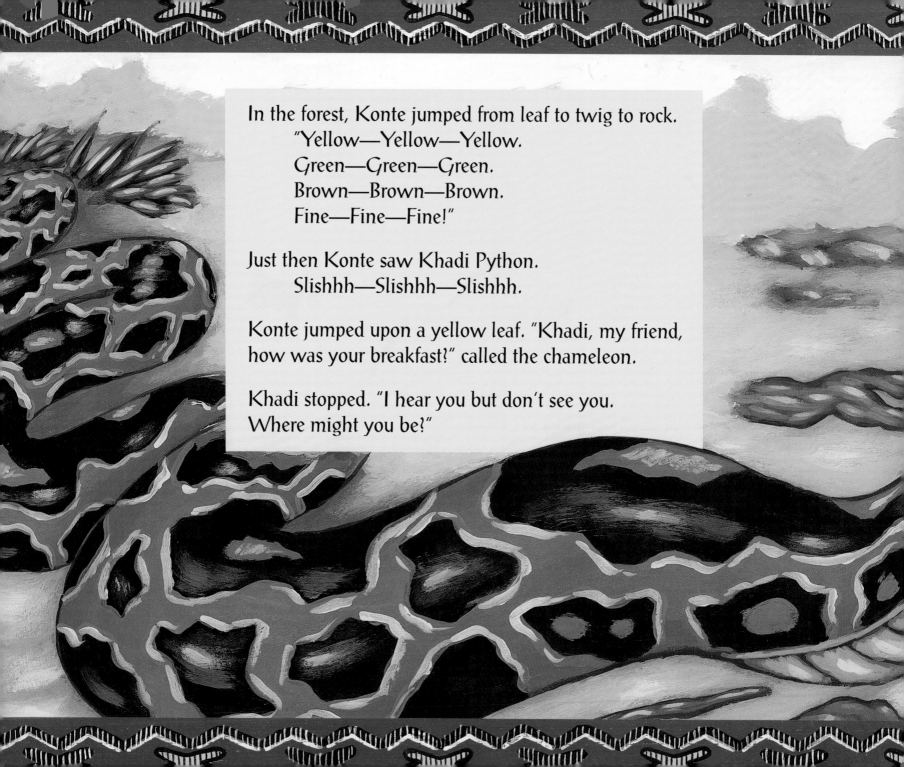

In the forest, Konte jumped from leaf to twig to rock.
   "Yellow—Yellow—Yellow.
   Green—Green—Green.
   Brown—Brown—Brown.
   Fine—Fine—Fine!"

Just then Konte saw Khadi Python.
   Slishhh—Slishhh—Slishhh.

Konte jumped upon a yellow leaf. "Khadi, my friend,
how was your breakfast?" called the chameleon.

Khadi stopped. "I hear you but don't see you.
Where might you be?"

Konte stepped off the leaf.
    Eho—Eho—Eho.

"Here I am," said the laughing lizard.

"Well, well. So you are," said Khadi, slissshhhhing away.
    Eho—Eho—Eho!

"If I can fool my friends, then I can fool my enemies.
No more running away. No more dinners that escape me."
    Eho—Eho—Eho!

Above the Buzza-Click-Fa-rump of bees, crickets, and frogs rose the laugh of Konte Chameleon. "Oh yes, life is suddenly much easier, for I will never have to hurry again."

Climbing a tall baobob tree dancing in the warm African breeze, Konte Chameleon said happily, "Yes, today looks like a good, good day. And I feel FINE, FINE, FINE!"

AUTHOR'S NOTE

My friend Yao Gozo told me this folktale while we were in Niger. The exact origin of the story is hard to determine. Yao is from Togo, and his grandfather, who told him the story, is from Sierra Leone, two countries in West Africa.

Yao's grandfather was a traditional medicine man who traveled the west coast of Africa selling his medicine in the markets. After years of journeys through Sierra Leone, Liberia, the Ivory Coast, and Ghana, he finally settled on the coast of Togo. Yao is not sure where his grandfather first heard the tale.

When Yao was a child, he spent many afternoons on the beach with his grandfather, listening to his stories as they crushed roots, leaves, and animal parts for his grandfather's medicine collection. The story of Konte was his favorite. He tells the story to his children today. Now I have told you. And so the tale of the chameleon continues to live and travel.

—Cristina